This Little Tiger
book belongs to:

For Laurence
~ CL
For Diane, Grahame
and Amy
~ GH

LITTLE TIGER PRESS
An imprint of Magi Publications
1 The Coda Centre, 189 Munster Road, London SW6 6AW
www.littletigerpress.com
This edition first published 2002
Originally published in Great Britain 2000
Text © Christine Leeson 2000
Illustrations © Gaby Hansen 2000
Christine Leeson and Gaby Hansen have asserted their rights
to be identified as the author and illustrator of this work under
the Copyright, Designs and Patents Act, 1988.
Printed in Dubai by Oriental Press
All rights reserved • ISBN 1 85430 681 2
1 3 5 7 9 10 8 6 4 2

THE GIFT OF CHRISTMAS

Christine Leeson   Gaby Hansen

LITTLE TIGER PRESS
London

It was Molly Mouse's first Christmas. The sky was streaked with pink and gold, and there was a tingle in the air.

Through the window of a house something shone out and glittered in the night.
"What is it, Mum?" squeaked Molly.
"It's called a Christmas tree," said her mother.
"People cover it with shiny balls, lights and stars."
"I wish *we* had a Christmas tree," sighed Molly.
"Why not go into the woods to find one?" said her mum. "You could make it look just as pretty as that tree in the window."

Molly thought this was a wonderful idea. She called her brothers and sisters, and off they all scampered.

On the way they came to a barn and the mice rummaged through it, looking for something to add to their tree. Under a big pile of hay, Molly found a doll.
"This is like the one on the top of the Christmas tree in the window," she said. "It will be just right for our tree."

But the doll already had an owner.

"Grrrh!" said the old farm dog. "That's mine!"

"Don't chase us!" cried Molly. "I only thought the doll would be nice for our Christmas tree."

The old dog yawned. Sometimes, it was true, he did chase mice. But maybe because it was Christmas, or maybe because he was remembering the time when he'd played with the children by the farmhouse Christmas tree, he said the mice could borrow his toy.

The mice left the farmyard, carrying the doll, and reached the edge of the wood.
"Hey, I've found something else to put on our tree!" Molly shouted.
It was a silver ribbon, hanging from a branch of an oak tree. Molly scampered up the trunk, took hold of the ribbon and pulled . . .

but the ribbon belonged to a magpie.
She had taken it to line her nest.
"Please don't be cross," pleaded Molly.
"I only wanted something for our
Christmas tree."

Now usually the magpie chased mice. But maybe because it was Christmas, or maybe because she too had also been admiring the Christmas tree in the window, she let go of the other end of the ribbon and Molly took it away.

In the distance Molly saw some red shiny things
lying on the ground. They were like the balls on
the Christmas tree in the window.
"Exactly what we want!" cried Molly, running
to pick one of them up. "Now we have a doll,
a silver ribbon and a shiny ball!"

But the shiny balls belonged to a fox. "Those are my crab apples," he barked. "I'm burying them for the cold days ahead."

"We only thought one would look good on our Christmas tree," said Molly, trembling.

The fox sniffed. He chased mice more often than not. But maybe because it was Christmas, or maybe because he had never seen a Christmas tree before, he went back into the woods, letting Molly pick up a crab apple and carry it away.

Twilight was falling as the mice went deeper into
the woods. There, in the middle of a bramble bush,
they could see a lovely shining star and a dozen
tiny lights glittering green and gold.
"Stars for our tree!" shouted Molly. "Let me get
them." But when the little mouse reached into the
bush, she found, not stars . . .

but a collar, belonging to an angry mother cat.
She had her kittens with her and their three pairs
of eyes shone in the dark.
"Oh dear!" gulped Molly. "I only wanted something
sparkly for our Christmas tree."
The cat pricked her ears. She always chased mice.
But maybe because it was Christmas, or maybe
because she remembered the Christmas tree in the
warm place where she'd been born, she slipped off
her old collar and let the mice take it away.

At last, in a clearing in the very
deepest part of the wood, the mice
found a large green tree. "Our
Christmas tree!" cried Molly.
On its branches they hung
the doll, the ribbon, the crab
apple and the cat's collar.

"Oh," said Molly when
they had finished.
"It doesn't look a bit
like the tree I saw."
Sadly the mice
turned away and,
disappointed,
went all the way
home to bed.

In the middle of the night Mother Mouse
woke up her little ones.
"Come with me," she whispered. "I have
something to show you."
Molly and her brothers and sisters scurried along
behind their mother, past the farm and into the woods.
Sometimes other animals hurried on ahead of them,
deep into the deepest part of the wood.

At last the mice reached the clearing
where the green tree grew. Molly stood
completely still. Her eyes grew round
and shiny.
"Oh, look at that!" she cried.

During the night the animals had all added
more decorations to the tree. The frost had
come and touched everything with glitter.
The little tree sparkled and shone and even
the stars seemed to be caught in its branches,
with the biggest and brightest star right at
the very top.
"Our tree is even better than the one in the
window," whispered Molly, happily.

And maybe because it was Christmas all
the animals sat quietly around at peace
with each other.

Books to put some sparkle in your day!

Where's my Mummy?
Jo Brown

The Wish Cat
Ragnhild Scamell
Gaby Hansen

Mouse, Mole and the Falling Star
A.H. Benjamin
John Bendall-Brunello

Smoky Dragons
Jane Clarke
Illustrated by Ben Cort

Can't you sleep, Dotty?
Tim Warnes

Fireman PiggyWiggy
Christyan and Diane Fox

For information regarding any of the above titles or
for our catalogue, please contact us: Little Tiger Press,
1 The Coda Centre, 189 Munster Road,
London SW6 6AW Tel: 020 7385 6333
Fax: 020 7385 7333
E-mail: info@littletiger.co.uk
www.littletigerpress.com